Bramble Bear

Pretends to be...

BRIMAX

"I don't like shopping!" said Bramble Bear. But then he saw a big crowd. Everyone was clapping and cheering and taking photographs.

"Oh, look! Billy Bear, the singer, is opening a new store," said Bramble's mother. "He's very famous!"

"I know!" said Bramble, as he waited for Billy Bear's autograph.

This book belongs to

....

Illustrated by Pamela Storey
Original story by Geoffrey Alan
Adapted by Lynne Gibbs

Published in Great Britain by Brimax Publishing Ltd
Appledram Barns, Chichester PO20 7EQ
Published in the US by Byeway Books Inc,
Lenexa KS 66219 Tel 866.4BYEWAY
www.byewaybooks.com

Printed in China

"If I were famous, everyone would ask for my autograph, too!" said Bramble.

Back home, Bramble decided to become a singer! He quickly searched for his toy guitar. One of the strings was broken, but that didn't matter.

Then Bramble put on his dad's old sunglasses. He thought they looked really cool.

Bramble used a plank of wood and two upturned buckets to make a stage. Then, strumming his guitar, Bramble sang and danced.

Suddenly, the plank and the buckets began to wobble, until... **crash!** Bramble wobbled right off!

"Why were you flying through the air?" asked Betsy Bear, who heard the crash.

Betsy had given Bramble an idea. He would become a famous flyer!

The little bear made some wings. Then he told Betsy to fetch their friends to watch 'The Famous Flying Bear'!

At the top of a hill, Bramble put on his wings – and began to run.

"Ooh, I feel dizzy!" gulped Bramble. "I don't think I will fly too high today."

Suddenly, a big gust of wind caught Bramble's wings and blew him up into the air! **Whoooosh!**

Bramble spun round and round, and down and down – until **SPLAT!** He spun into one of his friends, who was eating an ice cream cone!

"All flights are off!" groaned Bramble, lying on the grass with a big blob of runny ice cream on his head!

Covered in chocolate ice cream, mud and grass, Bramble went home.

"Oh, dear! What have you been doing?" asked Bramble's mother.

"I have been trying to become famous, but it's very hard work!" said Bramble, sadly.

But Bramble had an idea when he saw his mother's washing line.

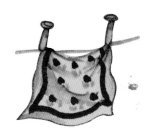

Bramble Bear was going to become
a famous tight-rope walker!

As his friends watched, Bramble climbed
a step-ladder to reach the washing line.

"I'll use this long cane to help me
balance," said Bramble.

But as soon as he stepped on to the
wibbly-wobbly washing line, Bramble
lost his balance – and tumbled off!

"Perhaps he's fallen in there?" said a rabbit, pointing to a bulging pillow case hanging on the line.

"At least you had a nice, soft landing," laughed some rabbits, as Bramble poked his head out of the pillow case.

"Huh!" said Bramble. "I don't like singing and dancing, or flying – and tight-rope walking is a very silly thing to do!"

"Come and see Bramble, the famous bear, row to the other bank in record time!" called Bramble.

Climbing into a rowing boat, Bramble said, "Start the clock, Betsy!"

But Bramble had forgotten to untie the boat – and began rowing round and round in circles!

"Oh, dear!" sighed Bramble's friends.

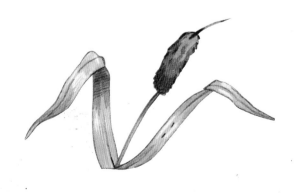

"It's no good!" sobbed Bramble, when his dad came along. "I'll never be famous."

"But you already are!" said Betsy. "There isn't another bear in the world who does all the things you do."

"You're right!" said Bramble, smiling. "I really am famous, after all! Now, would anyone like my autograph?"

What can you see?

Can you point to these pictures as you find them in the story?

sunglasses

guitar

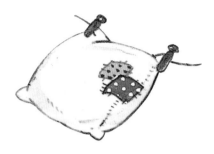

pillow case

washing line

bucket

ice-cream